COSCOM
ENTERTAINMENT

ALSO BY A.P. FUCHS

BLOOD OF MY WORLD TRILOGY

DISCOVERY OF DEATH
MEMORIES OF DEATH
LIFE OF DEATH

UNDEAD WORLD TRILOGY

BLOOD OF THE DEAD
POSSESSION OF THE DEAD
REDEMPTION OF THE DEAD

THE AXIOM-MAN™ SAGA
(LISTED IN READING ORDER)

AXIOM-MAN
EPISODE NO. 0: FIRST NIGHT OUT
DOORWAY OF DARKNESS
EPISODE NO. 1: THE DEAD LAND
CITY OF RUIN
EPISODE NO. 2: UNDERGROUND CRUSADE
OUTLAW
EPISODE NO. 3: RUMBLINGS
OF MAGIC AND MEN (COMIC BOOK)

MECH APOCALYPSE

MECH APOCALYPSE

OTHER FICTION

A STRANGER DEAD
A RED DARK NIGHT
APRIL (WRITING AS PETER FOX)
MAGIC MAN (DELUXE CHAPBOOK)
THE WAY OF THE FOG (THE ARK OF LIGHT VOL. 1)
DEVIL'S PLAYGROUND (WRITTEN WITH KEITH GOUVEIA)
ON HELL'S WINGS (WRITTEN WITH KEITH GOUVEIA)

Zombie Fight Night: Battles of the Dead
Magic Man Plus 15 Tales of Terror
Undeniable
The Dance of Mervo and Father Clown

Anthologies (as editor)

Dead Science
Elements of the Fantastic
Vicious Verses and Reanimated Rhymes: Zany Zombie
Poetry for the Undead Head
Metahumans vs the Undead
Bigfoot Terror Tales Vol. 1 (with Eric S. Brown)
Bigfoot Terror Tales Vol. 2 (with Eric S. Brown)
Metahumans vs Werewolves

Non-fiction

Book Marketing for the
Financially-challenged Author
Canadian Scribbler: Collected Letters of an
Underground Writer
Look, Up on the Screen! The Big Book of
Superhero Movie Reviews
Getting Down and Digital: How to Self-publish
Your Book
The Canister X Transmission: Year One

Poetry

The Hand I've Been Dealt
Haunted Melodies and Other Dark Poems
Still About A Girl

WWW.CANISTERX.COM

EPISODE No. 3

AXIOM-MAN™
RUMBLINGS

by

A.P. FUCHS

COSCOM ENTERTAINMENT

WINNIPEG

ISBN 978-1-927339-59-6

Published by COSCOM ENTERTAINMENT

Check out AXIOM-MAN on the web at
www.canisterx.com

Text set in Garamond; Printed and Bound in the USA

COVER ART BY JUSTIN SHAUF AND KYLE ZAJAC

To Andrew Lorenz, a longtime fan, reader and, now, a
good friend. Keep bringing on the superheroes, buddy.
I'll try and keep up.

This one's for you.

IT BEGINS.

AGAIN.

WELCOME TO THE pivot point, dear reader. Starting in this tale and for the three that follow it, *The Axiom-man Saga* as you know it will change forever. It's been nine years since the first book was released, and everything that has occurred until now has led to this moment. What you hold in your hands is the stage-setter for what's to come, the prequel to the *Battle of Power Trilogy*. Once concluded, the storyline that began in book one all those years ago will be finished and I'll be moving on to the second phase in the saga. Don't worry, the Axiom-man you know and love will still be present, but he will be different. Everything that he's experienced will influence what will take place in this book and the trilogy to follow. Everything hinted at or revealed will come into play. This has been planned from the beginning.

As the writer of the series, it's been a long road, longer if you include the creation of Axiom-man back when I was in high school. Even further if you add when I came up with the mythology when I was around nine years old.

Thank you for being on this journey with me. Thank you for letting me tell you a superhero tale that's meant so much to me over the years and reflects a great deal of who I am. If it wasn't for superheroes, I wouldn't be writing today. Definitely not. Like I've mentioned elsewhere, everything I've created is a superhero story in some way whether overtly or subtly. It's the genre above all genres and the greatest arena to work in as far as I'm concerned. It's an honor to share these tales with you and bring you along for the ride.

My hope is you have been entertained by the saga thus far, that you feel rooted in Axiom-man and all he stands for, and that, going forward, everything that's happened so far will carry weight and presence into what's to come.

The plan for a fifty-book series is still in place: twenty-five novels, twenty-five episodes, each release alternating between the two.

We're concluding the beginning of the saga starting this book here. I know the middle. I know the end.

Let's get there together.

Something is coming.

Something is rumbling.

Everything's about to change.

- A.P. Fuchs
Winnipeg, MB
October 18, 2015

Axiom-Man™
Rumblings

CHAPTER ONE

THIS HAPPENS FAR too often, Axiom-man thought as he lifted his face from the pavement.

Head swimming, he had to blink a few times to focus his vision.

Grunting, he got himself onto his hands and knees, then quickly collapsed, his limbs hollow, strength gone.

Whatever hit him, it got him good.

The last thing he remembered was flying over the city on a nightly patrol, his eyes keen on any suspicious activity in the yellow of the streetlights beneath him. The next thing . . . a pinch in his shoulder. Shadows rimmed his vision and the lights went out.

Now it was day and he didn't know where he was. Perhaps somewhere else in the city. Who or what brought him here, he didn't know. Quickly, he touched his mask to make sure it was still in place. There was nothing but fabric. He breathed a sigh of relief and realized his powers were still activated. Perhaps it was a side effect from the last surge he experienced; even unconscious, the power still coursed through him. Which was good, because that meant even if someone removed his mask, all they'd see was a man with blue hair. And if they checked his eyes, they'd see the luminance of blue energy crackling over them.

The faint blue aura that was also part of the upgrade from the last surge still glowed above his costume. Since the surge happened, he'd tested the aura and quickly learned that while it didn't make him indestructible, it added a level of shielding to his body, enabling him to take harder blows, even withstand bladed attacks provided there wasn't severe force behind them.

Axiom-man got back onto his hands and knees, this time more steady. He must've been drugged, some sort of tranquilizer that penetrated his aura and stole him from the sky.

His eyes ached with fatigue; he clenched his fist and forced himself to get up. Once standing on shaking legs, he took in his surroundings: a residential street, one he didn't recognize.

Time to get his bearings.

Vision still blurry, Axiom-man raised his eyes to the sky and ascended, the street below quickly shrinking beneath him.

There was black in his vision, a grid-like pattern. The drug? A hallucination? He shook his head a couple of times to try and straighten himself out, only to find his vision clearing and the grid still remaining in view.

Furrowing his brow, he stopped his ascent and floated in the air. Below, there were six streets, maybe around a kilometer long each, all parallel to each other, all residential. Reminded him of the neighborhood he grew up in. Right next to the streets was a small town. Well, not really. More as if a chunk of a city had been cropped from a metropolis of some kind and planted right beside the residential streets. He counted a few rows of that, each with buildings of various sizes but none containing anything monumental like a skyscraper. Axiom-man guessed the tallest building of the lot was around six or seven stories high.

Above him, the grid covered the city and residential streets like a dome.

RUMBLINGS

Weird, he thought. *Oh well. Doesn't matter. I'm outta here.* He flew up and headed straight for the grid. Knowing not to carelessly fly into it, he stopped just short of the thing and took a closer look. Each section of the grid was roughly four feet square. There didn't appear to be any glass or mesh or covering bridging the sections. As far as he could tell, it was clear through to the other side.

Silence hung on the air, everything about this place completely peaceful. He also noticed there was no wind.

Carefully, he floated toward the grid and slowly went to pass in between the structure's black metallic piping.

The moment he was flush with the pipes, a violent electric charge encompassed him, causing every muscle to cramp, like his whole body was making a fist.

Shouting, his brain quickly depleted of all thought, Axiom-man dropped from the sky and tumbled toward the ground below.

His body still contracting, he had enough of his senses intact to slow his rapid descent and bring himself to a halt mid-air. He remained hovering for several minutes, body shaking. Each time he stretched out his arms or moved his legs, his muscles revolted in pain. Heart racing, he finally caught his breath and simply did his best to slow down, calm down—relax.

Finally, the pain subsided. Fatigue filled his muscles from the sudden exertion.

"Okay, be careful," he whispered to himself and flew ahead to where the grid came down on the other side of the miniature city. This time he touched down and stood before it. Like it had been in the sky, the grid didn't display any sort of obstruction. Each section just looked like a square window frame.

You're gonna hate yourself for this, he thought. But he had to be sure. He reached out and felt the space between the frames.

Nothing.

Don't think you're so lucky. He'd probably just missed it.

Axiom-man took a step closer and reached out again. At first he thought he was in the clear, but once his fingers extended a few more inches, a violent jolt shot through his arm, causing him to snap his hand back and stumble a few steps, his muscles locked from fingertips to his shoulder.

"Ow!" He couldn't help but shout the word. Despite all the pain he'd been through in his career in the cape, this was still brutal.

Okay. Clearly every space between the gridlines is electrified. And, if there are a few holes, I'm not going to fly around and try every one. Would kill myself in the process. He had hoped that maybe this second time trying the grid, if he was careful, his aura might protect him. Perhaps it did a little, perhaps not. He didn't know its strength against electricity.

Hmm, feels like something out of Bleaken's playbook. But if Bleaken was responsible this place would be covered in dark cloud not an electric grid.

The ground beneath his feet was mere earth.

"Dig my way under?" he said.

Axiom-man got down on his knees near one of the gridlines and started digging where it met the ground, careful not to touch it. He got a couple of feet down; the piping was embedded deep in the earth. How far it went down was anyone's guess, but he supposed it had to be pretty deep to anchor such a huge structure. He just hoped all that was beneath the ground were support beams and nothing else.

RUMBLINGS

Once he dug as deep as his arm would reach, Axiom-man floated off the ground and fired up his eye beams. Giving it all he had, he at first took a shot at the space between the gridlines, thinking maybe he could blast through the electric field. His energy beams simply crackled against the field like water splashing against a window.

"Fine." Aiming his beams downward, he cut into the ground, blasting a hole as deep as he was tall. He kept going, getting some thirty or forty feet down. Loud cracks and pops coming from beneath the earth told him to stop. Maybe he'd hit water or a pipe or something.

Axiom-man dove into the hole, flying toward its bottom. He used the glow of his eye beams to see; there was nothing but earth around and beneath him.

Not bad. Will just touch down, aim straight, dig my way out the other side, all the way to China if I have to.

He landed and the moment his feet hit the earth, a huge electric blast pumped its way up his legs, causing his whole body to shake and jolt. He rebounded into the air, slamming into the side of the makeshift tunnel and scraping himself against the dirt as he made his way back to the surface. He came out of the hole and lay on the ground beside it, convulsing.

As his eyes began to close, he assumed the entire underside of this place was also guarded.

It was a cell.

CHAPTER TWO

JACK BE NIMBLE, Jack be quick . . . Jacqueline thought as she hopped from counter to counter in the jewelry store.

Thin and limber, bypassing the sensors on the floor was easy. Just stay on the counters. Fortunately, she barely weighed a hundred pounds and if she displaced her weight just right, she wouldn't risk breaking the glass of the display counters. Getting in here had been a little tricky, but after some nightly reconnaissance, she noticed every time old man Taylor closed up the shop, he'd close the door then open it a crack as if checking all was in order inside before locking it. She knew there was an alarm, but, it seemed, the door had to be opened a good way for it to kick in. Busting the lock on the outside door had been a snap—an old trick she learned a long time ago—and, thanks to her size, she was able to squeeze in between the door and frame without tripping the alarm. Because of gymnastics since she was a kid, she even did so without touching the floor and instead used the frame as leverage to get herself onto the countertop immediately to the right of the door.

As much as she hated clichés, she knew she was living one right now: a stealthy cat burglar clad in black head to toe breaking into a jewelry store. The thing was, gold and silver—and especially diamonds—were much more valuable than cash or any other electronic gizmo she could get from breaking into a box store. Besides, getting in and out of places like that was old news and no longer a challenge. Even home invasions had lost their charm. The only time things got exciting was when she didn't schedule correctly and someone had been home. Even then, a quick run through the house while they were chasing her and calling the cops let her grab a few trinkets on the way out. But there was no payoff in those, at least, nothing sustainable.

Truth be told, it wasn't even about the loot—as fun as its yield could be—but about the adrenaline dump from being in a place you didn't belong and doing something you weren't supposed to do.

Jacqueline—Jackie—eyed the diamond and gold rings beneath her gloved hands and booted feet as she moved about the counters. The displays were locked and a couple of laser sensors ran through them. Any attempt to break in and grab a handful of goodies would set off the alarm.

No matter.

She wasn't here for those anyway.

Old man Taylor had something better in the safe in the back room. As thorough as the old fella was at securing the place, he was a fool when it came to non-disclosure. Despite his age, the old timer kept a blog, one for collectors of old coins, jewelry and rare gems. Often he'd post pics of his latest find and do a write-up about each one. The item that caught Jackie's eye was a pair of emeralds the size of golf balls. She'd been in this shop several times—often wearing various disguises so as to not tip off the old man—and not once did she see the gems. This left only two options: either Mr. Taylor had the goods here, locked up and secure, or kept them at home. Given the security of his shop, she doubted his house would be outfitted with the same.

Though, she was aware, she could be wrong.

Now on the counter near the door to the back room, Jackie leaned over and pulled her lock pick from her back pocket. She inserted it into the knob, pushed, and maneuvered it around, getting the tumblers to fall into place. She worked it until the lock clicked. She checked out the rest of the door. Nothing around its borders indicated any further security. She supposed Taylor trusted the rest of the shop to protect it.

She slowly turned the knob and pushed the door open. The back office, which she had caught a look at during working hours, was simple: a desk with a computer for paperwork, a couple pictures of naval ships on the wall, and a safe in the corner.

Jackie stood on the edge of the counter and counted to three. She jumped off and caught herself between the doorframe, her feet still not touching the ground. With another jump, she pushed off the frame and landed on the desk, quiet as a cat. She stepped onto the chair then crossed over so she was crouched atop the safe.

Now to get in, she thought. This was the tricky part. The thing was made of pure steel. It wasn't a modern safe—which was odd in light of the tech guarding the rest of the place—but it wasn't an antique either.

"All right. Now it's smash-and-grab time," she whispered. From her inner jacket pocket, she produced a small packet of explosives. It was crude and homemade, but it packed a bang. She inserted it where the bolt met the frame near the locking mechanism and ran the wick out. A quick flick of the lighter got the thing going and the wick sizzled as the fire consumed it.

She covered her ears.

A loud bang echoed in the room when the flame found pay dirt, blowing the lock and bending the metal. The door hadn't blown completely open, so she pulled out a crowbar and went to work old school, prying at the remainder. Once done, she got out her flashlight and leaned over the edge of the safe and peered inside. Some stocks and bonds, a couple stacks of cash, a bag of gold rings, some old coins and a couple of unlabeled boxes of other stuff. On the bottom shelf was a black velvet box. She pulled it out and opened it.

Empty. Just two vacant holes where the emeralds should have been.

"Aw nuts," she said.

The office light went on. "Aw nuts is right."

CHAPTER THREE

AXIOM-MAN TOOK TO the sky and once again surveyed his surroundings, namely the outer perimeter to the place. If indeed the whole landscape was made to keep people in, there was little use in trying every square on the grid or blasting up the ground around its edges. But the amount of engineering it would take to totally lock this place down—maybe in the middle of the cut-out city the ground was grid-free?

Might as well try, he thought. Quickly, he swooped down and landed where the residential section met the buildings. There was road here and, he assumed, was manufactured no differently than any other road elsewhere. With a blast of his eye beams, Axiom-man got to work chewing up the cement and breaking through to the gravel beneath. He blasted past that and soon tore up the sand and earth under it. He floated upward to get a better angle then gave it all he had and ripped into the ground, flying into the hole until he was plenty deep like before.

"Now the fun part," he muttered. "Better not kill myself doing this." Careful this time, he righted himself then slowly floated toward the bottom of the hole, hoping the glow coming off his eyes would illuminate whatever was beneath him. Just moist earth. Slowly, he lowered himself then braced for a jolt when his feet touched bottom. The moment he touched down, severe tingling when through him, causing his muscles to quake and whole body to shake. Immediately, he floated upward. He hadn't dug deep enough to hit the grid proper, but there was no doubt the electric fencing was under the ground here, too.

Axiom-man flew to the surface and rose above the city.

Rat in a cage, he thought.

However, it seemed unlikely the whole complex was completely sealed off. Surely there was a way to get in and out. Whoever built this place would have to perform maintenance of some kind and had to be able to access the necessary tools or equipment to do so.

So, what, am I supposed to go through every house and building and try and find a way out? Seemed likely. It would also take him a day or more to do it if he checked out every nook and cranny. Worse, if this place was meant to be a fortified compound and keep people in, then there was a good chance any exit would be cleverly concealed.

He flew up near the grid and began lapping the area, keeping himself in line with the gridline and shape of the dome. Beyond the grid's holes on all sides was nothing but the gold of sand as far as the eye could see. If he was still in the province, he figured he might be around Shilo, perhaps near the military base up there. The more he thought about it, the more it made sense. This kind of setting would be consistent with a military exercise, a fake residential zone and city streets for soldiers to train in should they ever be called for civil unrest.

Now Axiom-man wondered if this was a military experiment or containment of some kind: lock him in a cage and see what happened.

By the time he was done flying around the perimeter and discovering no openings or gates of any kind, he had no choice but to start searching the homes and buildings. But which one? He tried to put himself in the shoes of those responsible for this, think how they'd think. The exit would be secret. Most likely in a place hard to get to. Then again, maybe that's what they wanted him to think. Perhaps the exit was in plain sight. Yet, if that was the case, they'd run the risk of their detainees finding it and getting out. Never mind the idea of the exit being concealed behind a wall or secret passage of some sort. What was he supposed to do? Fly around and blast everything to smithereens? He wasn't sure if he was alone or if anyone else was kept here. To destroy the homes and buildings could put others—*innocent* others—at risk. It could also nix any chance of finding an exit if he buried it beneath the rubble.

One by one it is, then, he thought, *starting downtown.*

Axiom-man took off for the buildings and did a quick sweep of the streets, getting a glance at the possibility of anyone else being down there. He turned up empty.

He kept it simple and started at the first building at the first row. It was five stories tall, a place reminding him of the old buildings in the Exchange District of downtown Winnipeg. Muddy red brick lined the outside. The windows didn't look new and had old trim. Perhaps some attention to vintage detail was given since the glass looked like salvaged material instead of something new. A double door was at the front of the place. Axiom-man took the handle in his gloved hand and gave it a tug. He found it locked.

Maybe I'll luck out and this will be it, he thought. The door could be locked for a reason.

Gripping the handle tight, he put his strength into it and ripped the deadbolt clean from its housing and got the door open. Tiles lined the flooring within, the walls painted white. Even the walls looked weathered. He was in a foyer. No furniture or carpeting. Hallways branched off to either side, dim lighting lining the roof and showing the way. No surprise the power was on. If you kept an electric grid running, might as well go all out.

He walked the hallways of the first floor, opening the doors to the various rooms that ran off it. This place was meant to mimic an old office building, he figured, but very loosely. Most of the rooms were empty. Some had old desks from the seventies and eighties in them, a few vintage chairs. One even had an old coffee maker on the table. While in each room, he did the same thing: first, eye the place down; second, start tapping the walls to test hollow points, even stomp on the floor in a few places to see if there was a gap beneath the tiling somewhere; third, take his fist to the walls and bust up the bricks and wood in places to see if there was a panel or door on the other side. In the rooms that had windows he'd step up to the glass and look out on the off chance the window itself was a fake despite the ones lining the outside. All of them looked out into the street beyond.

By the time he'd finished searching the first floor, he turned up nothing.

He had no choice but to keep moving and search the floor above him in case the exit was somewhere up there and, through its own network behind the walls, led to the world outside the grid.

The first building was a wash. Just the same thing on every floor: old rooms, walls with nothing behind them, windows looking outside. Axiom-man even punched through parts of the ceiling in case something was up there. Nothing. He double checked the first floor for a basement entrance but found none. Now outside, he sighed as he looked down the street and the buildings lining it. Despite working as quickly as he could, the first building took around three quarters of an hour. A bigger building would take longer. Then there were the houses to worry about. Worse, this whole search could be a fool's errand and there'd be nothing anywhere.

He chased the thought from his mind.

If they got me in here, there has to be a way out . . . unless the grid is the doorway, he thought. *Go in and out between the piping before firing up the electric field.* If that was the case, then he was screwed.

Heart heavy, he proceeded down the line and entered the second building, this one a story taller than the first. Interestingly, the door wasn't locked on this one. It was more modern, too.

"Let's get it done," he whispered, and got to work.

Chapter Four

The girls were always his weak spot. Their bodies—works of art, so simple yet so elegant. Even the most visually unsettling women had their strong points, and it was Bryce Carter's eye to pick out the beauty in women that was also his bane. That's why he was in the basement of Dave's Bar, sitting down with a cold pint at a small table while ogling the girl on stage. The basement was supposed to be a VIP area, but Dave's wasn't a place for VIPs. It could never be that classy. The bar's idea of a VIP area was simply tracking the high spenders upstairs and, if they were consistent enough with their excessive money dumping, invite them to come downstairs for some entertainment and higher end drinks. Down here, the beers were imports, the liquor a minimum of ten years old. Fancy, but *Dave's* fancy. Anywhere else, this would just be your average bar. Even the décor matched the upstairs. Was just better kept and the wood of the tables polished to a shine.

Bryce eyed the girl on stage. Madeline was dancing. She moved to the music with an energetic beat to her step, her feet hopping while everything else above her knees slowed down like flesh made liquid. Her long black hair drove him crazy, but the distant gaze in her eyes made her lack an appeal that otherwise would have gotten his attention.

But for Bryce, it was never about stereotypical primal hots for a girl. It was about appreciating their beauty for what it was, each woman a masterpiece even if sometimes it took him a while to figure out what the artist was trying to say.

He sat hunched over his table, pint in one hand, cigarette in the other. You could smoke down here despite the bylaw banning it everywhere else. Dave or whoever must've paid off the right people to avoid fines. He remembered the good old days when you could legally smoke in a bar, each cigarette going down as quickly and smoothly as a glass of rum.

He'd need another beer soon as this one was almost out. He didn't worry about the calories like some of the other guys he knew. Standing six-six and weighing in at around two-eighty, his body needed the energy even if it was from the sugar in the brew. He also worked out like a mad man, pumping iron in his dingy apartment whenever he got the chance. It wasn't even the earned strength that he did it for or the aesthetics—he was built more like strong man than a body builder anyway—but the high he got after setting the iron down. The endorphin rush afterward fired him up and made him feel like he could conquer the world.

But Bryce was no conqueror. He was a manual labor man, odd-jobbing it over the years and doing grunt work like hauling steel. He dropped out of school in ninth grade and had no qualifications other than being a package of muscle. Needed heavy work done? Bryce was your man. Needed someone to calculate a problem or strategically solve an issue? Call someone else. Bryce was far from stupid, but he tended to use his hands more than his head.

That was also why he was down here tonight. The VIP basement of Dave's Bar was ripe with cocky shmucks who thought they were a big deal because they were asked to come down here and have a few while taking in the sights.

Madeline's song ended. So did her set. She scooped up her stuff in her arms and walked off the stage to the hooting and hollering of the slobbering idiots in the crowd. The next girl came on, music blaring, and quickly started dancing.

Bryce pulled his eyes away from the dancer and surveyed the tables, searching for tonight's pickings. There was a couple in the corner, oblivious to everyone else, minding their own. A set of dudes sat across from each other in a booth and yacked away, a couple rows of empty glasses in front of them. Other men and women were scattered about the place, some just sitting quietly, eyes on their glass, others with eyes on the stage. A group of loudmouths were in the corner, whistling and chirping at the girl on stage while she provided them with cheap entertainment.

Bryce counted them.

Five.

All around six feet tall, probably a two-hundred-pound weight average between them.

Just the group he was looking for.

The waitress came by and Bryce gave her a couple of fives and ordered a shot and a brew. He lit up a fresh cigarette and smoked it while he waited for her to bring back the drinks.

The yahoos in the corner approached the stage in twos, talking filthy to the girl while slugging back their beers. She ignored them like a seasoned pro and kept on with her routine. Even the guys close to the stage seeing this said nothing; all part of a night at Dave's.

The waitress brought Bryce his drinks and he immediately shot back the bourbon and followed it up with a healthy swig of beer.

A couple of songs later, the girl's set ended and she got her things and headed off the stage. At that moment, one of the guys from the group hopped on the stage and started a show of his own. His buddy standing on the ground started to laugh, downed the rest of his beer, then dropped the bottle to the floor. The glass shattered, causing a couple of heads to turn but no one to move. The guy got on stage too and snuck in behind the curtain and pulled the girl back on. She shrieked and started hitting him, telling him to bug off.

"That's my cue," Bryce said and glugged down his beer. He crunched his cigarette in his hand, ignoring the burn. He was simply going to pick a fight with these guys and here they were giving him an excuse to pound their heads in before the bouncers got involved, which they soon would be since they were approaching the stage.

Bryce hopped onto the front of the stage and slugged the guy dancing there. He dropped him straight away, his meaty fist an easy weapon against the dude's face. The guy's friend stopped harassing the girl, let go of her, fear in his eyes. It was clear the guy hadn't thought this through. The man moved to get off the stage but Bryce grabbed him before he could. He spun the guy around so he faced his friends then quickly took the guy's head and smashed it into his knee. The crunch of the guy's nose breaking against it gave Bryce a thrill. He pulled the guy's head back and slammed him backward against the ground, smashing the rear of his skull into the stage. He faced the crowd and the three remaining friends. Though they hadn't done anything, he couldn't let the opportunity go to waste. They were standing right there, dumbfounded. He jumped off the stage, arms outspread, and tackled the group to the floor. He stomped on one guy's face while landing with an elbow to another's chest. He rolled on top of the third, straddled him, and pummelled his face to a pulp. The other two rolled around on the ground. Blood on his hands, Bryce pounced on one of them and made him taste it by punching him so hard in the mouth he knocked through his teeth, the thumb of his fist resting on the guy's tongue. He ripped his hand free, smacked the guy once more, then moved over to the last who moaned and groaned on the floor.

The bouncers—two big black dudes—were only a couple feet away. They appeared to be taking their time, enjoying the show.

Bryce grabbed the guy on the ground by the hair, pulled his head up, then smashed it back into the floor, cracking the skull. Blood rimmed the guy's head like a growing syrupy halo.

The bouncers grabbed Bryce from behind.

"Okay, that's enough fun," one of them said.

But it wasn't. Not yet.

Bryce pulled the two men together, smashing them into each other, then elbowed each in the face before letting go. The two men staggered back, each hunched over from the blow. Bryce jumped and brought a fist down on the back of each of the men's heads and turned the lights out on them.

He faced the onlookers in the room.

"All right, who else wants to party?" he said. He singled a guy out on his right. "You!" he said, pointing.

The man shook in his seat as Bryce marched over to him. Bryce stared him down at first, then, not taking his eyes off him, took the man's beer and chugged it down.

"Thanks," he said, setting the glass down. Bryce turned away and felt the man's relief send a sickening feeling down his spine. Quickly, Bryce spun back around, grabbed the guy by the head and smashed his face down on the glass. Wood cracked from the impact and blood ran off the table.

With a grin, Bryce cracked his knuckles, gave the stunned girl on stage a wink, then headed for the door. The moment he stepped outside, he was greeted by a pair of squad cars, lights flashing. Four cops. Two with guns drawn. Two with tasers.

"Evening, officers," he said. "Is there a problem?"

———

Bryce sat alone in a small room at the police station, hands cuffed to the table. The officers with the tasers wouldn't have been an issue, but the ones with the guns would've dropped him pretty quick. He was actually hoping he would've been able to finish his workout on them, but he didn't feel like getting shot tonight. When that happened—which it had during other brawls—the adrenaline dump wasn't always a pleasant high. Sometimes he lost track of himself and became a spectator to his own actions. Sometimes it got him in trouble, like the time he took on two loan sharks after one shot him in the arm but failed to see the other behind him who took a baseball bat to his legs.

A camera stared down at him from the corner of the room.

Looking at it dead on, Bryce said, "You gonna talk to me or what?"

The camera stared back.

"Pansies."

A couple of minutes later, the door opened and an officer let in a man in a fancy suit. He sat down across from Bryce and placed his briefcase on the table.

"So, what, are you my attorney?" Bryce asked.

"Something like that," the man said. "I'm here to make you a deal."

CHAPTER FIVE

THE SUN WAS setting by the time Axiom-man finished searching the buildings. It had been a useless pursuit. Even the building with the basement and metal square plate on the floor proved frivolous. For a second he thought he'd found a secret hatch, but it was just an opening to access some pipes, which were dry.

Now, once again standing near the hole he had blasted between the buildings and the residential zone, he found himself second guessing his work. Had he been thorough enough? Should he have taken down more of the walls? Torn up more chunks of the floor? He had looked everywhere for any sign of some sort of door or hatch or panel, only to find nothing more than your standard building infrastructure. Oddly, he thought, if he was being monitored, no one had come out to stop him from destroying pieces of this place. It made him wonder if he was truly alone here, just left by himself for who knew what intention.

There would be no sleep tonight. Not here. Which made for a long day since he'd been up early the day before and had gone out on his nightly patrol on top of that. Without having a day job anymore, he had more time to be in the mask. He just hoped the sleep he had thanks to the drug that knocked him out was enough to rest him up for what was no doubt going to be a long night ahead. Fortunately, the houses were smaller so going through them shouldn't take as long. Even if he could finish by sunup or just before, he should still be in pretty good shape rest-wise for whatever else might come next.

Axiom-man flew to the first house, a two-storey with an entrance on the side. Like the first building, this one was locked. He put his shoulder into the door and broke the deadbolt from the jamb. He was immediately in a small kitchen. A fridge, a stove, a table and a couple of chairs. The lights were on in here, too. He checked the window above the sink, again making sure it wasn't just for show. It looked out into the backyard. Like he had in the building, he tapped along the walls and punched through the drywall in places. Nothing but framing, some insulation and wiring.

Two bedrooms ran off the kitchen. He checked out each. They both had a bed, a closet with a couple of shirts and pants, a dresser with empty drawers. Nothing on the walls. After breaking up the drywall on those, he proceeded to the living room that also ran off the kitchen. That yielded nothing as well, same with the bedroom and bathroom that ran off that. Against the living room's far wall were two sets of stairs, one leading up, one down. He headed downstairs first, coming into an unfinished basement with concrete walls and floor, an olive green washing machine and matching dryer off in the corner. Axiom-man punched through the concrete walls, only to find dirt on the other side of the foundation. He blasted into the floor, and simply because he hadn't done so in the buildings, dug deep only to find more of the electric grid far below. He sat on the ground outside the hole, knees drawn up, elbows resting on them, and bowed his head to recover from the shock. By the time he straightened up, he wasn't sure how much time had passed. He hoped he hadn't briefly passed out.

Axiom-man went up the stairs to the main level then ascended the stairs to the second. It was like a second house up here, mimicking a renting space with its own kitchenette, living room, bedroom and bathroom. Like he'd been doing all day, he went through each room and came up empty. Grimacing, he clenched his fists and flew straight up, breaking through the ceiling and tearing the roof open. High above the house, he shouted at the sky then dove down to the next place, making his own doorway by blasting a hole through the roof with his eye beams.

He'd tear this neighborhood apart to find a way out.

———

The sky was still dark by the time he was done, the cool night air refreshing as he stood outside the last and final house, the outside wall completely blown open revealing the kitchen beyond. Unless he missed something in all his searching, it was clear he wasn't meant to leave. Eyes to his boots, he turned away from the mess and walked out of the yard and onto the street beyond, which eventually gave way to the section of dirt rimming the perimeter of the dome.

He wanted to scream, call out to whomever did this. After having shouted to the heavens the first time, he immediately felt bad and realized maybe gauging his reaction to being locked up was what this was all about. He had to play it cool despite how he felt inside. Show whomever was looking on that he couldn't be broken.

Through the gridlines above, the multitude of stars shone against a blanket of navy shadow. The moon— almost full—was bright and crisp.

He had one last idea. Just came to him now. The spacing between the gridlines was electrified, but were the gridlines themselves? Frustration driving him, Axiom-man flew into the air and straight into the gridlines above. Before he made contact, he envisioned pushing against them, bending them, breaking through to the other side. He was quickly corrected the second he touched them and a blast of electricity sent him tumbling back to the ground below. He stopped himself just before hitting the ground, then let himself flop on the dirt in defeat. Every muscle ached and spasmed. He couldn't get up.

He'd ride the wave, then plan his next move.

CHAPTER SIX

THREE MONTHS AGO . . .

JACKIE HAD BEEN in a Winnipeg Police Service interrogation room but once, the only time she had been caught. She had gotten complacent in a series of debit card swipes that caught up to her, most of the cards tap-enabled. It was when the cashier at Giant Tiger noticed her multiples of similar looking cards in her purse did the eyebrows raise and a phone call was made. Police picked her up shortly after. Fortunately for her, she ditched the cards before pick up thus the lack of evidence setting her free.

This room was different than the one at the WPS. These walls were burgundy, with a gleaming polished oak table in the middle which she sat behind. A camera was in the top corner of the room, keeping an eye on her. A single chair was across from her, a door on her right, leading in.

She drummed her fingers on the table. She'd been sitting here for nearly an hour. If only she could pace to help pass the time, but pacing denoted nervousness and could tip off whomever was watching that she was indeed guilty. Though she had been caught red-handed, that was beside the point. If they didn't have anything substantial about tonight's break-in, she'd be out soon.

Jackie wouldn't have minded a glass of water, though.

Finally, the door opened and a tidy man in a navy Joseph Abboud suit entered, his trimmed brown hair slightly gelled, keeping it to the side. He had bright blue eyes, which she found striking. He sat across from her and laid a file on the table.

Here we go. Typical police drama, she thought. She decided to keep her mouth shut for the time being.

The man eyed her for a moment then opened the folder. The top page had her particulars on it, just the basics like her name, address, phone number, date of birth. He paused, as if making sure she knew he knew who she was.

He flipped the page, revealing a black and white photo of her entering the jewellery store. He paused here, too, again seeming to make sure she saw it. He flipped the photo over, revealing yet another, this one of the time she slipped into the back entrance of Tiffany's and made off with the cash box on the manager's desk. He flipped this one over as well; another photo, her leaving her apartment, clad in her B and E gear. More photos, more depictions of past crimes. Some were of her in her day-to-day wear, just minding her own, walking down the street.

Jackie inwardly groaned and steeled herself against the realization these guys knew everything. Had the cops been onto her the whole time and only now had busted her? Why hadn't they stopped her before? Not enough evidence? Seemed they had enough; they did have her pegged at each crime scene, except for her earlier ones. Those were absent, she noticed.

The man gathered up the photos and tidied them back into a pile. He closed the folder.

Bravo. You got me. Now what? she wondered.

The man folded his hands and leaned forward on his elbows, brow furrowed, as if he didn't know what to make of her.

He stared at her like that for what seemed an eternity. She so badly wanted to cry out, *What!*

Finally, he leaned back in his chair, but kept his hands on the table. From what she could tell, he was unarmed. Taking him out shouldn't be an issue unless he was trained. However, she couldn't be certain someone else wasn't on the other side of the door in case something went wrong.

"Jackie Jergens," the man finally said. His voice didn't sound like she'd expected. It was smooth, youthful. She had expected a gruff police voice.

She didn't reply.

He kept looking at her. He glanced once at the camera then back at her, holding her gaze.

"Jackie," he said. "You should be proud because you're the first person we've sat down here."

In this room? Was it newly renovated? she thought. It was a dumb thought and she felt like an idiot for thinking it.

"No reply?" he said. "That's fine, but I think you're going to want to talk soon."

Don't start the whole I'm-better-and-smarter-than-you routine with me.

"I assure you, when you hear what I have to say, you'll want to speak," he said.

She leaned back in her chair and crossed her arms.

He held her gaze another long moment, then said, "As you clearly saw, we've known about you for a long time. And, I've got to tell you, we're impressed. Very impressed. Out of your entire career as a cat burglar, you've only gotten caught once. No small feat. What makes you even more interesting is out of anyone we're aware of, you have the cleanest record, that is, no one knows who you are. Except us, of course, and the Winnipeg Police Service from that one time they got you. But in the grand picture of those who steal for a living, you've operated in the shadows, coming out only to snatch what you want, then retreat back into them without a trace. More specifically" —he straightened in his chair— "the types of theft you chose weren't just those of the common variety, like simply shoplifting. It seems you could've very well gone that route but instead you decided to challenge yourself and go after some big game. B and E in a residential environment is one thing, but on a commercial and private level? Something else, especially since the places you've been in and out of have sophisticated equipment to keep their doors and windows secure."

Okay. So tell me something I don't know, she thought. With the way the guy was talking, it was hard to tell if he was a cop or detective trying to be tough, or someone else entirely. They didn't take her here in a squad car, but that didn't mean they weren't police. Could've been a ghost vehicle.

"I think the question you should be asking yourself," he said, "is why did these people bring me in tonight of all nights? Why now instead of earlier? Why, even, now instead of later?"

He was right, she knew. Maybe she had crossed the line, *really* crossed it and they'd had enough of her shenanigans. Maybe it was time to get hauled in before she caused some serious trouble.

"Jackie," he said, "before I'm going to say anything further, I want to remind you of one thing: we know everything."

Obviously. She finally said, "I want a lawyer."

"They would be of no help to you here."

"I know my rights. I don't need to talk to you before speaking with an attorney."

"You tried that ploy in the past with the WPS and did it get you anywhere? Did they provide counsel? No. They had you and they knew it. They just couldn't make it stick."

"You speak of the WPS as if they're something else."

"They are."

"Then what are you? Some CSIS agent?"

"No. I'm not with the Canadian Security Intelligence Service."

Despite her heart picking up speed, she did her best to stay calm. Were these *other* law enforcement? Other criminals, even?

Boy, you really done it this time, she thought. "Then what are you? A super secret agency, the whole, you know, 'we're higher than the government' thing?"

He smirked. "No. But we are private and operate independently of outside firms."

She scratched her head. "Okay, enough with the cryptic responses. Just lay it on me straight. Am I in trouble?"

The man's face betrayed no emotion. "No."

"Then what do you want?"

"To give you a profound opportunity."

"To, what, work for you?"

"Yes."

"I ain't stealing for nobody."

"But you're so good at it."

She let the compliment hang on the air, not that she wanted it or needed it, but to see if the guy would follow up with anything else. He didn't.

"This is where you say, 'what's in it for me?'" he said.

"Seems you already said it."

"Aside from a substantial payday, we're prepared to give you something more than what mere money can buy."

She nodded at the folder. "Sweep that stuff under the rug?"

"No," he said, "this is our insurance. Say no to us and this goes to the authorities. I don't think they'd be too happy to see it, and I don't think you'd be too happy with the outcome."

I'm not going to jail, she thought. *No way.* She sighed. "What can you give me that, as you say, money can't buy?"

"In this case, two important things: freedom—aside from being on-call for us—and something to make your job easier."

"Police immunity?" The words unintentionally came out. When the man smirked again, she asked, "What's your name?"

"Gerhard."

"Gerhard what?"

"Just Gerhard."

"Right." She drawled the word. "So . . . Agent Gerhard?"

"No 'agent,' just Gerhard, please."

She nodded. "What do you want to give me in exchange for my services?"

"Have you ever heard of something called the Enhancer?" he asked.

"No."

Gerhard picked up the folder with the photos, got up from the table and went to the door. "Come with me."

After a forty-eight-hour fast and nearly just as much time prepping, Jackie was ready. So said the doctor leading the procedure anyway. He called himself—and was addressed as—Dr. Sumer, but Jackie wasn't sure if that was his real name or not. Didn't matter. Part of the condition of the procedure was limited knowledge on her end. After the first two or so hours of her briefing with Gerhard, it was clear to her whoever these people were wanted to hold all the cards. Problem was, it was true. They had all they needed on her to put her away for a long time if she didn't comply. It was odd, though, them wanting to help her.

More like use *me*, she thought.

In the end, the deal was simple: if she stole for them, she was handsomely compensated. She could live her life as she pleased wherever she pleased as long as she appeared within twenty-four hours of being summoned. Some exceptions might apply, they said, but they never specified what those were. It was her skills they were after, and it was this Enhancer that was going to make it all possible.

"To put it in layman's terms," Gerhard had said within the first few minutes of their briefing, "the Enhancer will enable you to do things normal people can't do."

"Like what?" she had asked.

He let out a deep breath. "That's the main issue. We can't guarantee exactly *what* it'll enable you to do."

"You're not making any sense."

"Putting it bluntly—superpowers. Like Axiom-man. Like Redsaw." His tone was curt.

"You mean flight? Lasers? All that?"

"Unknown."

"What do you mean, 'unknown'?"

"It means what the word means: we don't know."

"That's—"

"We don't know in that test subjects have reacted differently to the formula, each person manifesting special characteristics dependent on their genetics."

"Well . . . can't you find out what that means pertaining to me?"

"Sure, we could map you, analyze your DNA, your cells and more." He lowered his voice. "Which we've already done, by the way, long before we met you."

"How?"

"We've been in your apartment."

"You son of a—"

"Now, now. Listen. We have created a formula just for you, designed and catered to how we *want* you to react based on the information we have, but like all mutations and genetic changes, I'm warning you there is no guarantee what has been planned will occur."

"Which is?"

"The plan or the non-guarantee?"

"What do you think?"

He leaned in close and told her softly.

"Oh," she said. "Are you serious?"

"Very. Even . . . deadly."

The way he said that last word sent a chill down her spine. "Could I die?"

He waited a moment before answering. "There is a chance . . . but it is slim. In the end—again, to put it in layman's terms—and between you and me, I really don't like the scientific terms; can barely pronounce the words—we're going to deconstruct portions of your genetic code and rebuild them in accordance to what I've told you."

"So if it works . . . I'll have . . . superpowers?"

He nodded. "Yes."

The following two days were spent resting and being informed of what might go wrong and what these people were prepared to do to save her life should the worst happen. Part of it was warning the procedure would be extremely painful despite being put under for most of it. The anaesthetic, they said, would knock her out, but they didn't guarantee it would dull any pain. They wanted to keep the nervous system as sensitive as possible for monitoring purposes and any painkillers administered would hinder that.

For not the first time, Jackie wondered if she was doing the right thing. She knew it was the *wrong* thing, but perhaps for the right reasons. Her heart ached at the knowledge her life was no longer her own. Not for the next little while, anyway. Perhaps after this storm passed she might be able to reclaim her life, but until then, she was at the mercy of these people.

She mulled over what Gerhard told her would most likely happen if all went according to plan.

Just keep your eye on the target. Just like a job. No different. It's the outcome that matters, not getting there, she told herself.

Now, she lay on an operating table, her wrists and ankles bound, her head, too.

Dr. Sumer made the final preparations while out of her peripheral she saw Gerhard talking to a man in the corner. The other man was too far out of her view to see him and the two spoke too quietly for her to make out the words.

Dr. Sumer didn't speak as he plugged in I.V.s and monitors; it drove Jackie nuts.

"I could say anything to you, couldn't I," she said, "and you'd say nothing?" He kept about his work. "Hope your wife gets run over by a car."

Dr. Sumer didn't pay her any mind.

"Your shoe's untied," she said.

Same thing.

"Jerk."

"Dr. Sumer doesn't speak English," Gerhard said, coming up to her. He loomed over her and seemed overly tall from this angle.

"Should've told me that at the beginning," Jackie said.

"Must've slipped my mind."

You're a jerk, too. "Hey!" she yelped when the sharp prick of a needle pierced her arm.

"Just the anaesthetic," Gerhard said. "I'll be in the other room."

"The other . . ." But it was too late. Jackie's vision rimmed in black and her eyes closed.

Nothing but darkness, complete and utter pitch black. Full silence encompassed her.

Jackie tried to open her eyes but couldn't make the muscles work. She tried to move, but couldn't locate her arms, legs, even body.

Breathe, she told herself. And that ability, too, seemed to be gone.

Every sensation was gone.

Every single one . . . except . . . pain.

Sharp tearing ripped through her, somewhere deep inside. It was on the right, the left, down the middle, running deep.

It was all deep. The superficial sensation of her skin and tissue was completely absent . . . yet it felt like she was being stretched past the point of splitting apart.

In the darkness of her vision, tiny yellow stars went supernova, exploded across her sight and vanished into the inky abyss, over and over.

Humming droned deep in what she guessed were her ears, but the sound was so distant in one ear and so close in the other—always changing places—she wasn't sure where her ears even were.

Violent vibrations coursed through her and something lurched from her body, yanking her upward. It slammed back down into her and sent her tumbling into the dark.

Her head pounded like someone took a hammer to it, constantly beating the steel head against her skull until the bone broke and her brain leaked out.

Harsh gouges tore up and down her body; she convulsed then slipped away only to be reawaken by haunting visions of her flesh being peeled from her bones then laid back down again only to be ripped off once more.

Air! I need air! It wasn't even words, only sensation.

Pounding, deep and profound, raced up and down her body, unrelenting and unstoppable. To call out, to cry out—to scream.

But her voice was gone.

She was gone.

Jackie . . . was gone.

The voices came and went intermittently behind the haze of darkness. Eventually, her body found its way back to her.

She opened her eyes, time lost on her, just a sudden rush of being somewhere far gone then violently plunged into chrono reality.

"Help," Jackie rasped, a sharp prick in her throat. She tried swallowing; it was like trying to push down a stone.

"It's okay, Jackie," a man said. "Just rest."

She tried to speak and it was only when the lights went out again did she realize it was Gerhard who had told her to sleep.

Jackie awoke again, this time as if waking from a terrible night's sleep. Her eyes ached and she could barely move. All she wanted was to roll over and fall back asleep, but soon she realized where she was and what supposedly happened.

The room was dark, just a faint golden glow coming from a nightlight in the corner. The walls were blank. Just her, a bed, and some monitors beside her. Her vision was fuzzy so she couldn't clearly make out the words on the equipment. The sensations on her skin told her she was in a light gown with tubes connected to both of her hands and arms, a couple in her legs.

Back aching, she wondered how long she had been out for.

A familiar voice came from the shadows of the room. "Welcome back."

"Gerhard," she groaned.

"I'll let Dr. Sumer know you're awake. You had us worried. It's been two months."

CHAPTER SEVEN

HOVERING HIGH ABOVE the makeshift cityscape, Axiom-man took in his surroundings. It didn't take a genius to figure out what was going on: this was a test.

Below, with the structures divided between urban and suburban, the electric dome overhead—this was all a setup. It was something he pretty much knew from the start, but after trying to escape and finding no way out, it became clear his being here was only the beginning. If whomever trapped him simply wanted to see him find his way out of a tough situation, they would've dumped him in a maze or some sort of confinement. To put him on a stage like this, there was going to be more to it.

You can't just build this place without some help, Axiom-man thought. *Whomever set this up is someone or people with resources.*

Could be the military. If he was still in Manitoba, he was somewhere around Shilo and there was a base up there. He thought maybe the next phase would be soldiers storming the compound and putting up a fight. But Canadian soldiers were like law enforcement. They were supposed to be the good guys. A guerrilla group, maybe? No. They couldn't afford this unless they had some serious backing. Terrorists? That was possible. Those guys had their ugly tentacles spread all over the globe, a lot of them with government funding.

His heart sank at the prospect of the Canadian government somehow being behind this place. If they wanted to work with him, surely they would've just approached him, not kidnap him. And if they did kidnap him, that would mean the country leaders he had put his hope in were no better than the crooks and villains he fought daily.

At this point, there was only one option: wait. Whomever did this would show themselves eventually. Until then, he'd bide his time. Surely he was being watched.

————

"How's he doing?" the voice came over the speaker.

Gerhard studied the surrounding monitors, all with different shots of the partial city and surrounding neighborhood. Axiom-man floating in the air occupied the central monitor. "He's confirmed his confinement, so clearly not one to skim over a situation. He's learned to be thorough since his debut, it seems."

"Progress comes to everyone," the voice said.

"Indeed."

"And the grid?"

"Holding. He's attacked it a few times, all to no avail. Interestingly, that kind of voltage would've killed a normal man. Not at first, but after repeated attempts. He's resilient, that much is certain."

"Agreed, and this we knew."

"Should we move on to the second phase?"

"I'll be in shortly. In the meantime, let him recover. We want things to be as fair as possible."

"Understood."

Chapter Eight

THOSE ARE NICE walls, Bryce thought. The burgundy paint suited this place.

Suited him.

Reminded him of blood, and he sensed a lot of life-or-death decisions were made in rooms like these.

Blood was a funny substance. Put a drop of it on a white napkin and it was this gorgeous crimson red. Give a vial of it to the nurse and it looked as dark as molasses.

He preferred it on people's faces.

Like on the face of the guy sitting across from him if some headway wasn't made soon. The man was clearly trying to intimidate him, acting all superior, his fancy suit and tidy hair reeking of money. Whether he himself had it or the people he worked for, it didn't matter.

He had the kind of face Bryce wanted to punch.

"Mr. Carter," the man said, "let me be cl—"

"Look, cut the crap, brown nose. I know why I'm here."

"I don't think you do."

"Throw one too many punches and eventually people want you to stop."

"Oh, Mr. Carter, we don't want you to stop."

Bryce arced an eyebrow. "Come again?"

The man eyed him. "Gerhard. That's my name."

"Nice to meet you, Mr. Gerhard."

"Just Gerhard."

"Like the artist. Yeah, I read those funny books, too."

"And it seems we live in a funny book world, don't we?"

What was this guy driving at? Bryce nodded. "Things have certainly changed, yeah. Human beings ain't the only ones on this planet."

"Aliens. Interesting." Gerhard folded his hands and leaned closer. "That's your theory on guys like Axiom-man, Redsaw, Bleaken?"

"What else could they be? No human can do the stuff they can."

"You have a point, and to be honest, I'm not sure it's an invalid one."

Bryce waited a moment before speaking. "I like your suit. Don't see too many officers wearing fancy clothes like that."

Gerhard studied him. The man in the suit came across like someone who was a chameleon when it came to conversation: change the tone and delivery to suit the circumstance. "Ah, to be an officer of the law. Had dreams of that once. Didn't pan out."

"I noticed the tint on the windows on the way down here. That dark, kinda illegal. Could hardly see out."

"Was for your own good."

"Nice little squad of men to bring me in, too."

"We know you like to fight. It's what brings you here. See this folder?" Gerhard nodded to the manila folder beneath his fingertips. "It's loaded with pictures of you knocking guys' teeth out every chance you get."

"That don't scare me. Throw me in the pen and there'll be more meatheads to bust there."

"I know you wouldn't mind the chance. You're a fascinating man, Bryce Carter. Sure, you're big and you look tough, but you strike me as the kind of guy who has deep-rooted issues that you've taken upon yourself to work out. The kind of issues only violence can solve."

You don't know the half of it, Mister, Bryce thought. Not that he was crazy or had a temper. The fighting, the pain inflicted on others—it was inward anger at himself directed outward for catharsis. A failed marriage, a joe-jobbing career, a daughter that barely knew him, and a distaste for anyone else who seemed to have their crap together. It also helped he was big. He found that if he played the *dumb* card, most people didn't take him seriously, which in turn gave him the excuse to hurt them if they ever crossed him. It wasn't his fault people treated him differently just because they thought he was stupid. Superficial society, superficial world.

"I tend to look at it more as a challenge," Bryce said.

"Oh? How so? If it's challenges you're after, why not join a boxing gym or an organized fight club?"

"They don't organize fight clubs."

"I meant some mixed martial art. Train up and you could take on guys in the ring."

"My ring's the streets."

"Fighting is illegal."

"Depends on the circumstance."

"*Your* fighting is illegal."

"Matter of perspective. I only beat up those who have it coming. Call it my civic duty."

Gerhard sat back in his chair. Bryce never took his eyes off of him. After a moment of silence, Gerhard slightly nodded then said, "You're just the man we've been looking for."

"I see, and all this" —he glanced around the room— "is what? Some secret recruitment centre?"

"In a way."

"So not police."

"No."

"Government?"

"No."

"James Bond spy stuff?"

Gerhard smirked. "No."

"Then what?"

"Let me show you."

———

Bryce lay on the operating table. This "procedure" had thus far lasted two days. The blood test he gave, he didn't mind. The urine test wasn't his thing though.

He needed a beer, but that was off limits until after the process was done.

Gerhard had laid it out for him, exactly what they were going to do. They wanted to enhance him, give him the power needed to crack as many heads as he wanted with little chance of resistance. The city would be his octagon, he was told.

"You're missing the point," Bryce had told Gerhard during his briefing. "It's not just about fighting."

"Then what is it about?"

"You really wanna know?"

"Yes."

"Then stay with me because I'm going to use a big word: enlightenment."

"Enlightenment?"

"You want to look yourself in the eye, a fight's the best way to do that. You not only learn the deepest secrets about yourself, but about those you are facing off against."

"I can see that."

"Yeah, I bet you can."

It was evident Gerhard was frustrated with him because Bryce hadn't let the man gain an inch of power. It seemed Gerhard was a man who, while not the main mastermind behind all this, was still someone who liked control.

And Gerhard got it, because he said, "You're a dog, Mr. Carter, one that won't go on his leash."

"Thanks for the compliment."

"So we brought you a chain. You do as we say, you can fight anyone you want whenever you want. If you don't comply" —he tossed a picture on the table— "this one gets a bullet to the head."

The young, innocent girl in the photograph—his sweet, beautiful daughter, just turned four years old.

Bryce jumped up, reached across the table and pulled Gerhard onto it. "You son of a—"

The next instant, an electrical surge coursed through him and he let go.

Gerhard pulled back, taser ready. "Do that again, the next one's a bullet. Do you understand?"

Bryce didn't reply.

"Do you?"

Grimacing, Bryce pushed down the pain, the heartache. He couldn't risk dying. His little girl needed him, even if he was on the periphery. "I understand," he said softly.

Tears pricked at the corners of his eyes. His daughter, Sabrina, the only one in his life who could evoke an emotional response.

Oh, but to tear Gerhard's heart out, feel it pulse between his fingers . . .

Now, on the table, the doctor finished checking his vitals. Bryce didn't even want to know the guy's name and cut Gerhard short when he introduced him.

If this so-called procedure went to plan, Bryce vowed he'd free himself and Sabrina from those holding the chips. Until then, he'd bide his time. Play along. Have some fun. Get good at using whatever gifts this procedure was supposed to give him.

Gerhard came over to him. "All is ready?" He looked to the doctor, who nodded in return. "Excellent. I hope to see you on the other side."

Was that a joke? It was made clear he could die during this procedure.

The doctor hooked up the anaesthetic into the I.V.; it started to drip.

What if this whole thing was a joke? What if these guys were just thugs messing with him, some sort of elaborate revenge plot from those he'd beat up in the past? What if that picture of his daughter was just some sort of cruel ruse? What if—

Darkness.

Bryce was aware enough to study the black in front of him, to appreciate the silence all around. No sight, no sound, no sensation anywhere. And Time . . . there was no Time in this place. It was like a dream where all that mattered was the moment.

Heat swelled up somewhere below him, enrapturing what might've been his legs though he couldn't be sure. The heat spread and worked its way up toward his line of vision, splashing outward in searing flame, filling what he only guessed were his arms. His head went alight with blazing spikes of agony.

Bryce growled and screamed, though no sound came out of his mouth. The heat filled him, gave him form, ripped through his body like a rabid wolf tearing apart a lamb. Each slice of pain that tore through his limbs made him scream, pain crossing over into maddening ecstasy.

Is this it? Is this the best you got? Come on! Fire it up! Let's see what you— He screeched, his voice echoing in his own head, his heart, his soul.

Mental flashes of his limbs being torn from his body in glorious ribbons of flesh and splashes of blood filled his mind's eye then were quickly vanquished when a new rush of pain ripped through him.

A thousand pounds crushed every muscle and bone, and when the weight was just about to ebb, then came crashing down two thousand more.

He split apart, came back together.

His body tore left, it tore right.

Back as one unit, fire laced through every atom of his being and he violently convulsed in response.

He was everywhere in the dark.

He was nowhere.

Pain.

Screaming.

————

ONE MONTH AGO . . .

When the room came into view, Bryce welcomed the simple sight of the white-tiled ceiling.

His vision out of focus, it was hard to make out anything in this plain room. Nothing on the walls, nothing on the floor. Just him, the bed beneath him, a bunch of machines to his right and left.

"I'm alive. I made it," he rasped.

"You did indeed."

Bryce knew that voice. Gary? Garr—Gerhard. Yeah, that's it. Gerhard.

RUMBLINGS

Bryce's mouth was so dry it felt like it was filled with cotton. "What happened?" The words barely came.

"You just had the fight of your life. So far, anyway."

Chapter Nine

Today...

It was mid-morning. Axiom-man wandered up the main street of the small city, taking in the buildings from ground level. Maybe he had missed something? A sign? A clue? Anything that would indicate where he was or why he was here. Perhaps, even, who was behind this.

The night had been a long one. All he did was find a rooftop and waited.

His eyes ached for sleep.

The buildings were unlabeled. Not that that would've been necessary. He just thought maybe whoever constructed this place would try and make it more city-like by putting fake business labels on the buildings.

He paused when he caught a glimpse of someone up ahead, a shadow near the corner of a building that vanished quickly behind it.

"Hey!" Axiom-man took off, flying down the street full throttle. When he landed at the corner . . . he was too late. They were gone.

He glanced around. The street he had just flown down was empty. He looked up. Someone, clad in black, was on a rooftop across the way. He rose into the air and sped toward them. They vanished from the rooftop's edge just as he was nearly level with it. Once atop the building, he was alone again.

"Show yourself!" he shouted.

The rooftop remained empty.

He stood on the ledge, took in the city.

The person was on the street below, closer.

Female.

In a costume.

Axiom-man leaped off the ledge and kept his eyes fixed on her.

She turned to move away but he was beside her before she could go anywhere.

She wore all black, a half mask covering her face. Her hands were covered in long red gloves and black antennae sprouted from the top of her head. She wore something on her back, a black shell covered in large red spots.

"Nice costume," he said.

She sweetly smiled. "Do you like it?"

"I . . . guess." She was beautiful, at least from the part of her face he could see. Her outfit was also quite . . . complimenting. "Who are you?"

"Mmm . . . wouldn't you like to know."

"Where are we? Did someone kidn—"

Cutting him off, she stuck out her hand. "Name's Lady Fire."

"You look like a lady*bug*," he said.

She didn't say anything.

"Axiom-man," he said, taking her hand in his. The moment he made contact, a blast of flame shot forth from somewhere beneath her palm, the fire sending him flying back. When he hit the ground, he was glad to see the flame hadn't penetrated his aura.

She chuckled. "Lady *Fire*." She stretched out both hands and sent whirls of flame his way.

Axiom-man dove to the side, avoiding the blast. "Stop it!"

Lady Fire didn't pay him any mind and sent another stream of heat toward him. This time he took off into the air, flew around the line of fire, and came in from the side, tackling her to the ground. He had her pinned. All it would take would be a quick slug to her temple and she'd be out cold, but the way she looked at him, as if wanting him to do it, kept his hand at bay.

"I don't want to hurt you," he said.

"Because I'm a woman?"

That was true. Like most men, even if in danger, hitting a woman was a line he didn't want to cross. "Stop this. Let's talk."

She smiled that sweet smile again. "I'd love to, darling, I really would, but not today. Today I'm going to play hard-to-get."

"That's not what I—"

Lady Fire wrapped her legs around his waist and, with a quick twist, flipped him over so he was on the bottom. "I like wrestling. I see you do, too."

"Not really." He grabbed her by the shoulders and gave her a push. She fell backward, landing by his feet. He stood. "No more. Fair?"

She sighed. "No." Fire brewed beneath her hands and soon exploded his way. The blast of heat sent him backward.

Furrowing his brow, Axiom-man quickly moved out of the flame and ran toward her. He tackled her to the ground, one hand at her throat. He forced himself to raise his fist. "Last chance."

Her fist came in swiftly from the side, cracking him hard across the jaw. Another quick hit came in under his chin, snapping his mouth shut and slamming his teeth together. Lady Fire wormed out from under him, was on her feet inside of a second, and delivered a quick side kick to his chest. His aura absorbed most of the blow; either that or she didn't hit him very hard. But those fists . . .

Another round of flame swirled around him. He jumped into the sky only to glance down to see her flying after him, her shell now parted, wings revealed and ablur. It was hard to tell from his vantage point if the wings were mechanical or natural.

Natural? he thought. It *was* possible; he had seen stranger things since he first donned the cape and mask. And if it was true, she was certainly the first of her kind so far as he was aware.

He arced upward, the idea being to spike straight up, loop, then come in behind her to take her down. She followed his lead, mimicking the maneuver. Axiom-man dove downward, again attempting a loop which would get him in behind her. She followed suit.

"Okay, so she's good at flying," he muttered.

This time he dropped from the sky, turned around as he fell and aimed for her wings with his eye beams. The blast of blue energy from his eyes pierced the air and headed straight for her. She dodged the beam.

"Hey, no fair!" she said.

Axiom-man sent off several more blasts. Lady Fire flew in and around the attack, avoiding each one.

Another inferno exploded from her hands and came at him. The world lit up yellow and orange, temporarily blocking her from view. Axiom-man flew out of the flame, this time feeling some of the heat through his costume.

This aura thing was still new to him and he didn't know its limits. He suspected a sustained blast of fire would quickly penetrate it and he'd get burned.

He looked around. The sky was clear.

Where did she—

A violent blow struck him at the base of his skull and he lurched forward. Arms and legs wrapped around him from behind, jerked him backward, and the two ascended high into the sky.

He grabbed her arms, squeezing her hard so she couldn't release, and went nose-diving toward the ground.

"What are you doing?" she screamed.

He pressed his lips together and flew full tilt toward the ground. Lady Fire pulled against him, trying to let go. Axiom-man clung onto her hard. If she wanted to do this for real, he was going to give it to her. He hoped that, maybe, he could scare her instead of beating her up.

They were almost at the ground. Axiom-man flew hard then went parallel to the ground before impact. They sped just above the cement; with a quick jerk, Axiom-man flipped over so she was on the bottom and threw her arms off him and kicked free from her legs. He immediately slowed down while she skidded and rolled across the ground and crashed hard into a building wall.

Axiom-man flew over to where she lay in a heap.

Lady Fire's chest rose and fell.

Still breathing, he thought. *Good.*

Nothing seemed to be broken, nothing obvious.

He knelt down beside her and tilted her head so he had better access to her mask.

Just as he got his thumb underneath the material by her eyes, what felt like a freight train slammed into him.

CHAPTER TEN

IT FELT LIKE Axiom-man's skeleton went for a spin inside his body. The world reeled and his legs immediately went to rubber. One moment he was over Lady Fire, the next—a block away, sprawled out on the ground. Every muscle trembled from the impact and his left side was near numb.

When he stood, it was like holding still after spinning in circles. He teetered on his legs and when he righted himself enough to face the direction he'd come, he was greeted by a giant black fist to the forehead. The world flashed dark and pain went down from his head to his knees. Through blurry vision, he realized he was back on the ground, legs folded under him.

Towering over him was a behemoth of a man. The guy was at least six and a half feet tall, if not more, his wide frame at least double the width of his own. The guy wore a dark gray leather jacket, revealing a shirt with a giant yellow B emblazoned on it. He wore a matching bandit cap and a black domino mask. His handlebar mustache hid his age. A big black boot came stomping down toward Axiom-man, driven by gray-clad legs as wide as tree trunks. Axiom-man rolled to the side and felt the ground shake when the boot missed and made contact with the ground.

The guy's like a tank, Axiom-man thought. *And . . . in a costume.*

It was oddly comforting to meet these two, other costumed people. Aside from himself, Redsaw and Bleaken, there hadn't been anybody else wearing an outfit since he started this super-powered journey.

Unfortunately, thus far, it seemed everyone else wearing a costume was out to get him.

The man grunted and charged at him. Axiom-man leaped into the air and rose above his head, getting some distance.

"Get down!" the man yelled.

"No," Axiom-man said. His head still spun. "Who are you? What do you want?"

"Me? Nothin'." Then, as if to himself, "Well, that's not true. There's lots of things I want, but nothing from you."

"Then why—"

The man jumped, his mighty legs sending him high into the sky even as Axiom-man floated upward to get away from him. The man swung out and Axiom-man tucked up his legs beneath him, avoiding the blow. The fellow dropped from the air and landed back on his feet with a thud.

The guy eyed him then turned and went up the side of the street and ripped a lamppost from the ground. He maneuvered it in his hands as if merely adjusting a javelin; he hurled it at Axiom-man. The metal missile sped toward him; Axiom-man blasted a beam of energy right through it, splitting it in two.

The next thing he knew, a large dark blur was headed toward him: a car. It plowed into him, sending him flying back through the air, the momentum pinning the vehicle to him. As friction took over and the car slowed, Axiom-man pushed himself off it, flew over it, and stuck out his fists in front him. Kicking on the speed, he flew at him and slammed his fists into the man's chest. The guy folded in two as Axiom-man ran him over. Landing on the opposite side of him, Axiom-man turned to see the guy getting off the ground.

RUMBLINGS

I held back, not wanting to kill him, but he just took it, he thought.

The man dusted off his jacket. "Not bad," he said. "What else you got?"

Axiom-man quickly glanced around, looking for Lady Fire. Couldn't see her anywhere. He hoped she wasn't lurking nearby.

"I don't want to fight," Axiom-man said.

"But I do."

"Why?"

"Would you believe that, simply, I like it?"

"That's not a good enough re—"

The man charged at him again, his powerful legs propelling him in long leaps across the ground. Right when he was about to strike Axiom-man, Axiom-man once again rose into the air. The man dipped forward from the momentum of the missed blow, his fist smashing into the pavement, breaking it into huge chunks. Like a stone from a sling, the man threw a chunk of concrete at him, striking him in the legs.

The aura absorbed some of the blow, but Axiom-man's thigh muscles spasmed.

The guy was in the air in no time and plucked Axiom-man from thirty feet off the ground. The two fell and hit the pavement, the man on the bottom.

"Listen," Axiom-man said, "I—"

"Name's Battle Bruiser."

Battle Bruiser. Cute. It fits, though.

Battle Bruiser swung out and clocked Axiom-man across the face, sending him flying off. Axiom-man rolled across the ground, head ringing. He was pretty sure he felt blood leaking down somewhere by his eye beneath his mask. He hoped the damage wasn't too severe.

Can't take him head on, he thought. He wished he was trained to use another person's weight and strength against them. All he could do right now was try not to get killed.

He flew toward Battle Bruiser and slammed into him, tackling him to the ground. Once on top, he delivered blow after blow into the man's head, hoping to knock him out. The guy just took it, exchanging each blow for a grin. Axiom-man didn't even make him bleed.

A sharp pain hit Axiom-man in the small of his back when Battle Bruiser nailed his knee into him. Axiom-man's body locked up and he was effortlessly tossed off the man like a basketball thrown to the side.

He stood, feeling like he just had it out with a semi.

The Bruiser stepped toward him, cold eyes locked onto his.

Axiom-man fired off an energy beam at the man's feet in an effort to warn him off.

He kept coming.

Axiom-man did it again.

Didn't faze him.

Axiom-man shot off a beam directly at Battle Bruiser's chest, hoping to stun him. It had no effect.

"Hm, tingly," Battle Bruiser said.

"I'll give you tingly," Axiom-man muttered and gave the beams more power.

Battle Bruiser crossed his arms like a shield in front of him and pressed against the stream of energy coming at him. Axiom-man increased the beam's strength. Battle Bruiser planted his feet and leaned into it. Slowly, he began stepping forward, his pace quickening with each stride. Axiom-man put his heart into it and poured on the power. With a shout, Battle Bruiser pressed through and grabbed Axiom-man by the neck even with his eyes still ablaze with crackling blue energy. Within a second, Axiom-man spun in the air, eyes still alight, the energy beams cutting into the surrounding structures of concrete and glass. Quickly, he was through a window and skidding across the floor of what could've been an office space had this been real. He smashed through the drywall and finally stopped in the hallway beyond.

Hurting all over, Axiom-man lay in stunned awe at the man's strength. It was unlike anything he'd ever encountered before, not even from Redsaw.

There's no way I can beat him with brute force, he thought. He needed to outsmart him. The problem was, the guy was seemingly unstoppable.

Low thuds and crashing glass came from somewhere below him.

A moment later, a pair of hands burst through the floor and ripped him through it. He hit the ground on the level below. Battle Bruiser stood over him. With a quick snap of his fist, the Bruiser punched through the drywall beside him and ripped out a two-by-four from the frame and swung it like a baseball bat. A blast of energy from Axiom-man's eyes sent the beam in splinters.

Battle Bruiser lunged at him. Axiom-man flew up and out through the hole in the floor above and back the way he came when he first crashed through.

Back out in the city, shouting filled the air as Battle Bruiser came smashing through the third story window and landed in the street. He directly marched to another car—a Volkswagen—and sent it hurtling through the air. Axiom-man blasted it in half, transforming it into a fireball of debris.

Getting an idea, and hoping the guy was predictable, Axiom-man flew closer to him but kept himself out of arm's reach. When he was about twenty feet above the guy's head, Battle Bruiser leaped up to grab him. Axiom-man moved out of the way of the man's hands and plowed his fist as hard as he could into the man's face, hoping the impact of the strike *and* the guy's own upward momentum would double the impact. Battle Bruiser's head crunched into his neck and he fell to the street below.

When he hit the ground, he looked up at Axiom-man, seemingly stunned.

Axiom-man lit his eyes with crackling blue energy. "Ready to talk?"

CHAPTER ELEVEN

"Ladies first," Battle Bruiser said.

Nice, Axiom-man thought, thinking the guy was just being a smartass. Suddenly, flame engulfed him and it took him a second to realize what was going on. Axiom-man spun out of the heat, his skin beneath his costume warm from the blast.

Lady Fire flew in and capitalized on his being distracted by delivering two quick blows to his body before following up with a kick to his abdomen. On instinct, Axiom-man backhanded her and sent her tumbling through the air.

She slowed herself and rubbed away the blood leaking from her bottom lip. "Nice to see a real man has finally joined us."

Out of the corner of his eye, Axiom-man caught Battle Bruiser jumping up to grab him. He leaned into him, ramming his shoulder into the behemoth and knocking him back down to the ground.

Lady Fire flew at him and latched on, putting him in a bear hug. A massive spike of pain cracked through the top of Axiom-man's skull as Battle Bruiser jumped up and brought his fist down on top of Axiom-man's head. The world went dim and green fuzz rimmed Axiom-man's vision. Fire laced through his body and when he finally came around, he shoved Lady Fire off him and sent her to the ground below with a blast of energy from his eyes. He must've struck her too hard because she didn't move. He wasn't sure if she was out cold or not.

He slowly floated to the ground, too disoriented to stay in the air.

I have to get out of here or I'm going to get killed, he thought. The notion was barely coherent.

Battle Bruiser.

Where was—

Axiom-man's legs were swept out from underneath him and what felt like iron shackles wrapped around his ankles. He was spun around and around and hurled high into the air, heading straight for the gap between the grid dome. He put on the brakes and slowed himself to a stop before impact.

Two on one.

Two *meta*humans on one.

The only way to stop them would be to contain them, knock them out, or—though he hated to admit it—kill them. That last option wasn't on the table. He knew nothing about these two or why they were doing this. They could be acting against their own will so far as he knew.

But how to contain them? Lady Fire hadn't exhibited any supernatural strength. It was definitely enhanced, but it was nowhere near the power level Battle Bruiser showed. Trapping her somewhere was an option, but there was nothing in the faux city and residential area below that could hold Battle Bruiser.

Lady Fire flew up to meet him, sending off fireball after fireball in his direction. Axiom-man got his head together and dodged each strike, maneuvering around them in the air.

I'm so sorry, he thought. He was still hung up on hitting a woman despite striking her earlier.

He tried to grab her in the air so he could punch her out, but instead she flew around him and kicked him in the back. Compared to Battle Bruiser's, her blows barely made a dent

She flew into him, wailing at his face with her fists. He took a couple shots to the chin then swatted her hands out of the way and clocked her one good with a hook punch to the temple. She fell from the air. He chased after her, arms already outstretched to catch her.

Battle Bruiser beat him to it and jumped off a nearby rooftop and pulled her from the sky. Once the Bruiser set her down to safety, he turned his attention on Axiom-man and waved him downward.

Axiom-man flew off, hitting the residential zone, getting some distance and a few minutes to recover. Thankfully, the aura was protecting him enough that what he'd just gone through hadn't killed him. He just didn't know how much longer he could keep things up in spite of it.

Landing on a driveway, Axiom-man ducked in behind the car sitting there then discreetly made his way into the house. He quickly searched each room, hoping to find something—anything—he could use against this guy. The rooms were pretty much bare save for a bed without sheets, an old stove, a fridge and a toilet.

"Useless," he muttered.

A low rumble came from outside the house; Axiom-man couldn't quite place it but he knew what it meant. The booms got louder and the distinct sound of walls being smashed and wood and drywall crashing down grew clearer the closer the sound got.

Axiom-man readied himself and steeled himself against impact.

Battle Bruiser exploded through the living room wall, slightly adjusting his course so he could hit Axiom-man dead on.

Axiom-man lit up his eyes and unleashed his power as Battle Bruiser connected. As he took Axiom-man through the next wall, Axiom-man saw the tunnel of destruction the Bruiser had done to all the adjacent houses. The man was a machine.

Cranking up his power to its maximum, Axiom-man poured all he had into his energy beams. At first, it seemed as if they had no effect on Battle Bruiser, but after going through the fourth wall, the man finally began to slow down. Axiom-man adjusted his line of sight from the man's chest to his face and poured his power into him.

Battle Bruiser slowed right down and abruptly stopped. Axiom-man kept going despite smashing into another wall behind him. He didn't let up though and kept zapping Battle Bruiser with as much force as he could muster.

Soon the man started to flip out and smash and claw at the flooring around him, ripping up the carpet and wood until he fell through to the basement beneath.

Axiom-man came over and stood by the hole; Battle Bruiser shakily got to his feet.

Axiom-man fired into him, resolving to not stop until the man finally yielded.

A shocking impact burst through the back of Axiom-man's skull and in between his shoulder blades as a porcelain sink came down on him. He dropped and fell onto his side by the edge of the hole.

Lady Fire was back, baring her teeth, blood smudged around her lips.

Axiom-man lay there, catching his breath. "You got . . . to stop this."

"Why?" she said. "I'm having too much fun."

He needed another break, and he had to act soon lest he be drawn into another round of fighting he might not make it out of.

As fast as he could, Axiom-man got to his feet and flew straight up, smashing through the roof and emerging outside the house. Working as fast as he could, he flew up and down the breadth of the roof, smashing it in so it fell onto the two people below. It wouldn't hold Battle Bruiser, but it could put Lady Fire out of the picture for a while.

When done, he flew off back toward the city streets, getting as much distance from them as he possibly could.

Landing on the far side of the compound, he took a deep breath and coughed up a wad of blood. He tore a small hole at the bottom of his mask to let the goop out before once again taking in the electric grid surrounding this place. Between those electrified bars was his way out, but he'd already tried escaping that way. Even searched elsewhere in the city, even below it in places. The problem with the electric field was that when he struck it, it was like hitting a wall. It wasn't merely something you could pass through and endure a severe shock. Did that only apply to smaller objects like him? What if it was something bigger?

Axiom-man tore off back down the city streets, flying as fast as he could all the while keeping an eye out for Lady Fire and Battle Bruiser. It only took a minute for him to find what he had set out for: a small car. Better, he found a smart car. It should fit. He landed beside it, bent down, and picked it up from behind. Holding it tight, he took off back into the air and headed straight toward the grid near the ground. He kicked on the speed and revved things up to his max of a hundred kliks an hour.

He braced for impact.

The car smashed into the space between the grid, bright blue bolts of electricity shooting up and all around it, the car itself compressing on impact as if hitting a brick wall. A violent course of electricity conducted through the car, jolting Axiom-man's bones. He pulled his hands away and flew over to the side, his whole body shaking from the ordeal. He lay on the ground, trembling, forcing himself to ignore the pain. Behind him, the car cracked and popped as the electricity surged through it, eventually igniting the seats and dash within, engulfing the thing in flame.

The heat from the vehicle bonfire drew closer.

No, not the car.

Lady Fire.

Chapter Twelve

Axiom-man's cape was aflame.

He scrambled to his feet and ripped it off, tossing it to the side.

The aura didn't extend to the cape.

Lady Fire sent a stream of flame his way. He flew up then low, forcing her to momentarily lose her aim. He landed beside her and grabbed her by the wrists and drove them upward, the fire from just under her palms sent toward her face.

She shrieked.

"Leave her alone!" Battle Bruiser's voice boomed. He shoulder checked Axiom-man and sent him hurtling through the air. Axiom-man skidded across the roof of the fiery car and landed on the other side.

The crunch of metal followed as Battle Bruiser hoisted the car above his head. "I've always loved me a good fight," he said. "Too bad it has to end."

Axiom-man held his hands out in front of him as the car came crashing down. Within seconds, the heat from the burning metal began to permeate the aura. He couldn't press against the car to get it off him lest he risk searing his palms. Firing up his energy beams, he let them rip into the vehicle and blew the thing apart. He quickly rose into the air to get away from the heat.

Lady Fire flew up to meet him and let him have it with a kick to the head. The blow dazed him for a quick second. He reached out and grabbed her and threw her into Battle Bruiser, who had just jumped into the air, presumably to take him down. She smashed into him and the two dropped to the ground below. It was clear when

Lady Fire got to her feet she was shaky. For a second, Axiom-man thought she'd turn in place a couple of times before falling over. Battle Bruiser steadied her.

The big man got behind the girl and pointed her in Axiom-man's direction. He raised her hands toward him and fire poured out from beneath her palms. Axiom-man flew out of the way then circled down and sent off energy beams at her hands. She screamed and he hoped he had fried whatever tech gave her that fiery power. If it was tech.

Battle Bruiser ran at him. Before he hit him, Axiom-man saw Lady Fire try and send some heat his way but to no avail. Distracted, Battle Bruiser crashed into him and sent him flying backward. He landed just shy of the grid.

Soon both metas were heading right for him—Bruiser running, Lady Fire flying.

Just before Battle Bruiser made impact, Axiom-man leaped up and let the man crash into the grid. The electricity snapped and crackled all around him in a brilliant display of blue lightning. Lady Fire stopped just short of Axiom-man; not wasting a second, he spun in behind her and shoved her into Battle Bruiser. The two metas shook and quaked as the volts ran through them.

Battle Bruiser shoved Lady Fire away; she hit the ground, out cold. Axiom-man wasn't sure if she was dead.

With a growl, Battle Bruiser pulled himself away from the grid and took a step forward.

Axiom-man ran and kicked him back into it then fired his energy beams at him with all he had, keeping the guy in place.

Battle Bruiser shouted, begging Axiom-man to let him go.

Axiom-man didn't pay him any mind and kept firing away, vowing not to stop until the man ceased moving.

The surrounding grid area lit up in spiky electricity, its power keeping the Bruiser in place, shocking the life out of him.

Battle Bruiser screamed.

The grid cut out.

The man fell forward, his clothes nearly all burned off, his skin charred in multiple places.

It was over.

Carefully, Axiom-man approached the grid and put his hand out.

Nothing happened.

He stepped through. The elation . . .

Glancing back, he looked at Battle Bruiser's and Lady Fire's laying forms. He couldn't leave them here, but where could he contain them back in Winnipeg? Same facility as Bleaken? And he still didn't know how far from the city he was.

But he couldn't leave them here.

Maybe he could find something in the city in the dome to put them in, transport them both at once? But what if they came to while he had them? He'd have to fight them all over again and he could barely stand as it was. He certainly didn't want to sit and babysit them until someone came around. And that someone could be anyone, even a new meta.

He moved to go back inside the grid but was quickly shot back by a burst of electricity. He fired off a few eye blasts to the squares in the grid, each one blocked by the electric wall that was back online. There was no getting to the two people now.

The adrenaline pumping through him caused him to shake . . . as did the rage that someone captured him and put him up against these two.

He'd wait it out. Someone was bound to show up sometime.

———

Night had fallen when Axiom-man came to, lying outside the grid. All he remembered was getting dizzy and nearly every muscle in his body hurting in sharp bursts of pain. On the other side of the grid, Lady Fire and Battle Bruiser were gone. Collected or left on their own steam, it didn't matter now. The compound was quiet.

Pissed that he passed out, Axiom-man rose into the air and flew over and around the grid, looking through the gaps, hoping to see someone—even the two metas— in the city and housing within.

The streets were empty, nothing left but the aftermath of the fight he put up as two metahumans tried to kill him. Two metahumans he hadn't met before today and who seemed to have only wanted to have done him in for fun, no rhyme or reason.

The image of this place was burned in his mind's eye, though, and when he got back to the city, he'd alert the authorities of its whereabouts.

As he flew away, he wondered who had been behind the whole thing.

CHAPTER THIRTEEN

"ARE THEY CONTAINED?" he asked Gerhard.

"Yes, sir, of course. Back in holding. Once recovered, they will be released as per our agreement with them."

"Thank you for your assistance."

"You're welcome." Gerhard paused. "I hope it was fruitful for you."

Oscar Owen emerged from the shadows in the room. "It was. Rats in a maze. One got out."

"With all due respect, sir, you let him out."

"I didn't say how big the maze was, Gerhard."

"Sorry." Gerhard stood from his chair. "Is there anything else?"

"No. Thank you for coming. A car is waiting for you outside as per our arrangement. I'll take over from here."

Gerhard stuck out his hand. "Thank you for the opportunity. Please be sure to let me know if you need anything else in the future."

Oscar simply nodded and Gerhard left the room.

He went over to the monitoring station and eyed the different screens that showed images of the staged city and residential zone.

"He barely broke a thing," Oscar said to himself. It was evident Axiom-man had a respect for property and kept the damage to a minimum when it could be helped. Had there been people in this setup—even dummies— Oscar wondered how many might've succumbed to injury or worse.

It was Battle Bruiser who tore the place up. The man was a brute, nothing but raw power unleashed. Lady Fire was more careful, but Oscar wasn't convinced she had been so intentionally.

But Axiom-man—that's who this whole thing had been about. Oscar had gone toe-to-toe with him before, and the man in blue had great power though not as much as his own. However, it seemed things had changed since they last fought all out. It appeared Axiom-man had grown even stronger. He'd just taken a beating unlike anything Oscar had witnessed or dished out himself. Resiliency seemed to be one of Axiom-man's gifts.

The clock was ticking, however.

The being of shadow that visited him not long ago had relayed a message. Oscar's master wanted to break through and re-emerge. Earth would be the entry point, another Doorway.

But Axiom-man would need to be eliminated first.

For that, Oscar had a plan.

Axiom-man flew back into the city. He had been right. He had been up by Shilo. First stop was the police station.

Jack Gunn sat at his desk in the Special Force Unit, munching on a donut and sipping coffee. He was a mess of a man and an uncomfortable ally, but had proved to be one of the good guys despite rumors of the WPS having some of its people bought off by underworld authorities.

"You look like garbage," Jack told him as Axiom-man approached his desk.

"Not in the mood to trade insults, Jack," he said.

Jack took a bite of his donut. "Yeah, I can see that. Where's your cape?"

Axiom-man ignored him. "Was out west by Shilo. Someone locked me in a cage."

"Mm hmm. When?"

"About two days ago. Just spent all day fighting for my life. Met some new people. Your workload is about to get a lot bigger."

Jack slurped back the rest of his coffee then threw the Styrofoam cup toward the trash. It bounced off the rim. He didn't bother picking it up. "What people?"

Axiom-man filled him in.

"Great, just what we need," Jack muttered, "more freaks in a mask running around."

"At least this freak's on your side," he said, referring to himself.

"Yeah, well, we'll keep an eye out for them. It's all we can do. Can't do nothing until they make a move."

"Thanks."

"Besides," Jack said, "you better go recover or whatever. The radio's been filling up with alerts all over. Some of it's petty, but we got B and Es going down like we've never seen and a couple of bodies have shown up. These ones with burn marks."

"Redsaw?"

"Maybe. Aren't you the one who's supposed to be keeping tabs on him?"

"Like you, Jack, I only know something when I hear something."

Jack stood and put his hands on his hips. "Yeah, well, whatever. Go do what you gotta do and check back in the morning."

"Not taking orders from you."

"It's not an order." His expression softened. "It's simply a request."

Though he felt like hell, Axiom-man couldn't just lay low, not with the city acting up. "Give me a radio. I'll keep it on me. Drop me a line if you need my assistance."

"I said, come back in the morning."

"And I said give me a radio."

Jack coolly eyed him then searched his desk and the table behind it. "Jackass."

Axiom-man stared right back and didn't say anything when Jack passed him a radio. He merely turned and walked away.

CHAPTER FOURTEEN

AXIOM-MAN FLEW OVER the city.

More than anything he wanted to go home, tell Valerie he was all right, inspect the damage and crawl into bed.

But not tonight. Not after what Gunn said.

The city was acting up, more so than usual.

He flew over the Richardson Building; an illuminated figure stood upon its roof.

"Can't be . . ." Axiom-man whispered. He slowed down and descended. When he landed behind the figure, the messenger turned to him.

"My friend," the messenger said.

Axiom-man was at a loss for words. It had been a long time. He didn't know the messenger could simply show up; he always thought he had to be summoned via his computer.

The messenger reached out and put his hand on Axiom-man's shoulder. An electric warmth poured from his touch, soothing every aching muscle, sore joint, cut and bruise. When the messenger let go, Axiom-man felt much better. He knew the messenger had the power to heal. Tonight was a good night for compassion.

"What can I do for you?" Axiom-man asked.

The messenger's featureless illuminated face seemed to study him for a moment. "I come with a warning."

Great, more bad news. He thought maybe he should tell the messenger what just happened, but he knew better than to interrupt this being's course of conversation. "What kind of warning?"

"Redsaw's master is rising."

Axiom-man furrowed his brow. "I thought that was a long ways off? At least, that's how I understood it."

"Seems his cunning knows no bounds and he fooled us both. Darkness surges in the cosmic realm, its power growing with each passing moment. Earth is the gateway. You know what happened when Redsaw opened the Doorway of Darkness."

Axiom-man knew all too well: it broke open the boundaries between realities and allowed a supernatural fog to enter the world, the fog that created Bleaken.

"Where is he?" Axiom-man asked. "Where is Redsaw now?"

"Creating death wherever he goes. He's amassing power like before. Have you not noticed the rise in innocent deaths in your country?"

Axiom-man monitored the headlines regularly, but assumed the homicides abroad were products of man. "He did that?"

"Not all, but a large number of them. And look at where you've just been. Those two people, nearly killing you."

"What are they? Did the fog create them, too?"

"No. They were made by man. They were . . . enhanced."

"The Enhancer," he said. It was what he and Katie had dealt with in their dealings with the Russians.

"Your world is changing, Axiom-man, and the rate of transformation has increased one hundred fold. Unfortunately, humanity will fall unless we are prepared."

"We? You're going to join me this time?"

The messenger's light dimmed a little. "Not in the way you'd wish. Even in the way I'd wish. It is forbidden for me to interfere with what's to come, the reason of which will one day be revealed. I am a servant of a higher

Source, who knows all things. We must trust His wisdom. He's trusted me with you. So far, you have done well."

"When will this happen?"

"I do not have a specific timetable. I cannot give you a date. But what I can tell you is it will be soon. This world will be shaken and the battle you have been fighting will only grow."

"What about allies? Help? If I'm reading you right, this thing's going to be huge. How can I, just one man, stand strong? I barely survived the last forty-eight hours. Will there be another surge? Will I receive more power?" He hoped so. Just the thought of going up against Battle Bruiser another time made him sore all over again.

"You will receive what is needed when it is needed. Remember, you are but a vessel, a way to restore not only balance between Good and Evil, but to lead to the day Evil will be eliminated entirely."

"By fighting Redsaw, or his master."

"By continuing on the path you are on. You must trust my judgement. I want you to be ready hence my coming to you. The city will grow darker in the coming days and, shortly after, so will the world. Earth is your battleground, my friend. Stand tall, stand strong. Defend it." The messenger's light grew bright and he faded away.

Axiom-man took a breath. He had more questions. So many more. Why the guy couldn't stick around or talk straight to him, he didn't know. Perhaps part of this journey was to learn to figure things out for himself. It was being entrusted to *him* to come through, not the messenger.

A lot had happened since he first got his powers. His life had changed so much. So had the world. Redsaw's opening the Doorway changed everything as well. He'd just hoped he had more time.

But it seemed time was running out.

An explosion went off down the street, a flash of orange catching Axiom-man's attention. He radioed it in to the WPS then jumped off the building ledge, swooped down then flew toward the scene.

Screams for help and police sirens filled his ears.

Darkness was brewing.

Something was rumbling.

About the Author

A.P. Fuchs is the author of many novels and short stories. His most recent efforts of putting pen to paper are *Axiom-man Episode No. 3: Rumblings*, *The Dance of Mervo and Father Clown*, *The Canister X Transmission: Year One* and *Mech Apocalypse*.

Also a cartoonist, he is known for his superhero series, *The Axiom-man Saga*, both in novel and comic book format.

Fuchs's main website is **www.canisterx.com**

THE

CANISTER X TRANSMISSION

Get the newsletter weekly in your inbox

Also get the clown thriller
The Dance of Mervo and Father Clown **free**
as an eNovelette upon signup

www.tinyletter.com/apfuchs